TIFFANY STONE

KNOT CANNOT

ILLUSTRATED BY MIKE LOWERY

DIAL BOOKS FOR YOUNG READERS

For Banana, who is a snake, and Abby Ranger, who is not.
And to Kate Harrison, thanks . . . a lot!
-T.S.

To Aimee and Steph
-M.L.

Dial Books for Young Readers
An imprint of Penguin Random House LLC, New York

Visit us online at penguinrandomhouse.com

Printed in China
ISBN 9780735230804

10 9 8 7 6 5 4 3 2

Hand lettering by Mike Lowery
Design by Jasmin Rubero
Text set in KG Blank Space

THIS IS KNOT.

THIS IS NOT KNOT.

THIS IS SNAKE.

KNOT ACHES TO BE LIKE SNAKE.

SNAKE CAN SLITHER.

KNOT CANNOT.

SNAKE CAN
HISS.
YIKES
KNOT CANNOT.
BZZZ
OH NO, A GNAT!
HEY! GET OFF ME!

SNAKE CAN SWALLOW HER SUPPER WHOLE.

KNOT CANNOT.
(KNOT DOES NOT EAT SUPPER.)
I WISH I HAD A MOUTH.

SNAKE CAN EVEN SHED HER SKIN.

SNAKE LOOKS BRAND-NEW.

CAN KNOT LOOK BRAND-NEW?

NO, HE'S A FRAYED KNOT.

CAN KNOT
DO THIS?

HOP. HOP.

KNOT CANNOT.

CAN KNOT
DO THIS?

KNOT CANNOT.

KNOT BOBS.

CAN KNOT DO THIS?
KNOT CAN...
NOT.

WHAT CAN KNOT DO?

SNAKE TASTES THE AIR WITH HER TONGUE.
(NOT KNOT.)

OH NO!
DANGER!

BIRD LANDS NEARBY.

KNOT IS NOT AFRAID.

BIRD CANNOT SWALLOW KNOT

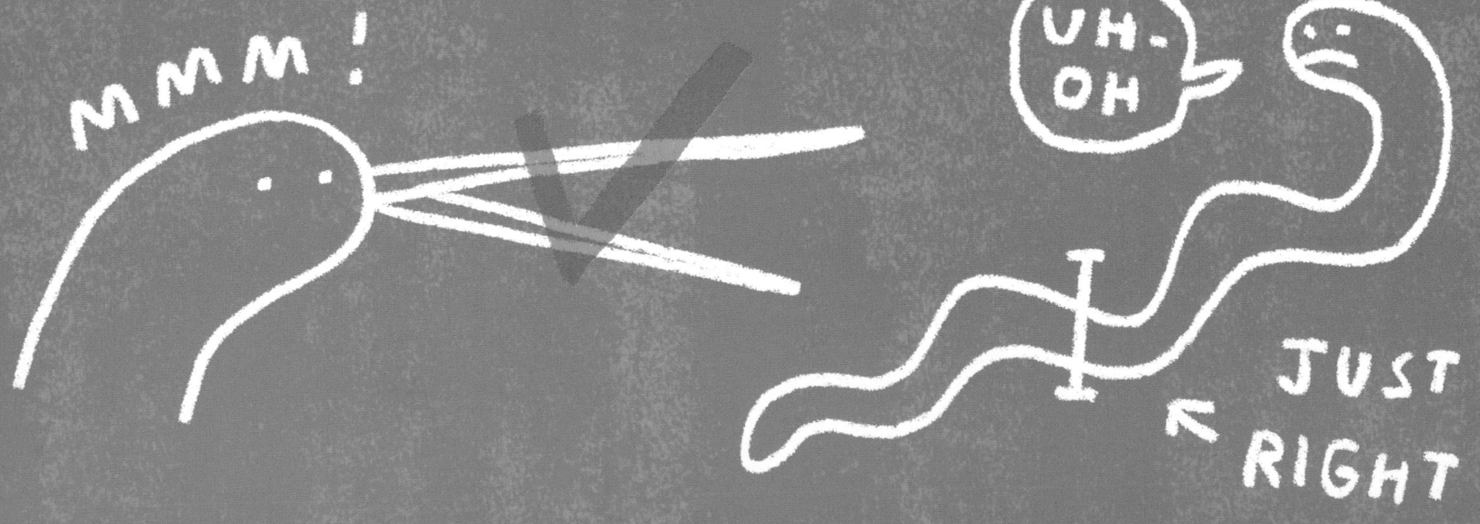

BUT BI[illegible]D CAN SW[illegible]LLO[illegible] [illegible]AKE.

SNAKE IS **AFRAID.**

SNAKE CANNOT ESCAPE.

KNOT

CAN...

KNOT!

BIRD CANNOT SWALLOW A GREAT BIG **KNOT**.

NOT BAD, KNOT.

KNOT STILL CANNOT **SLITHER.**

KNOT STILL CANNOT **HISS.**

KNOT STILL CANNOT SWALLOW HIS SUPPER **WHOLE.**

OR SHED HIS
SKIN.
OR
CLIMB
OR
SWIM
OR
BEND.
OR TASTE
DANGER.
WHAT CAN
KNOT DO?

KNOT...

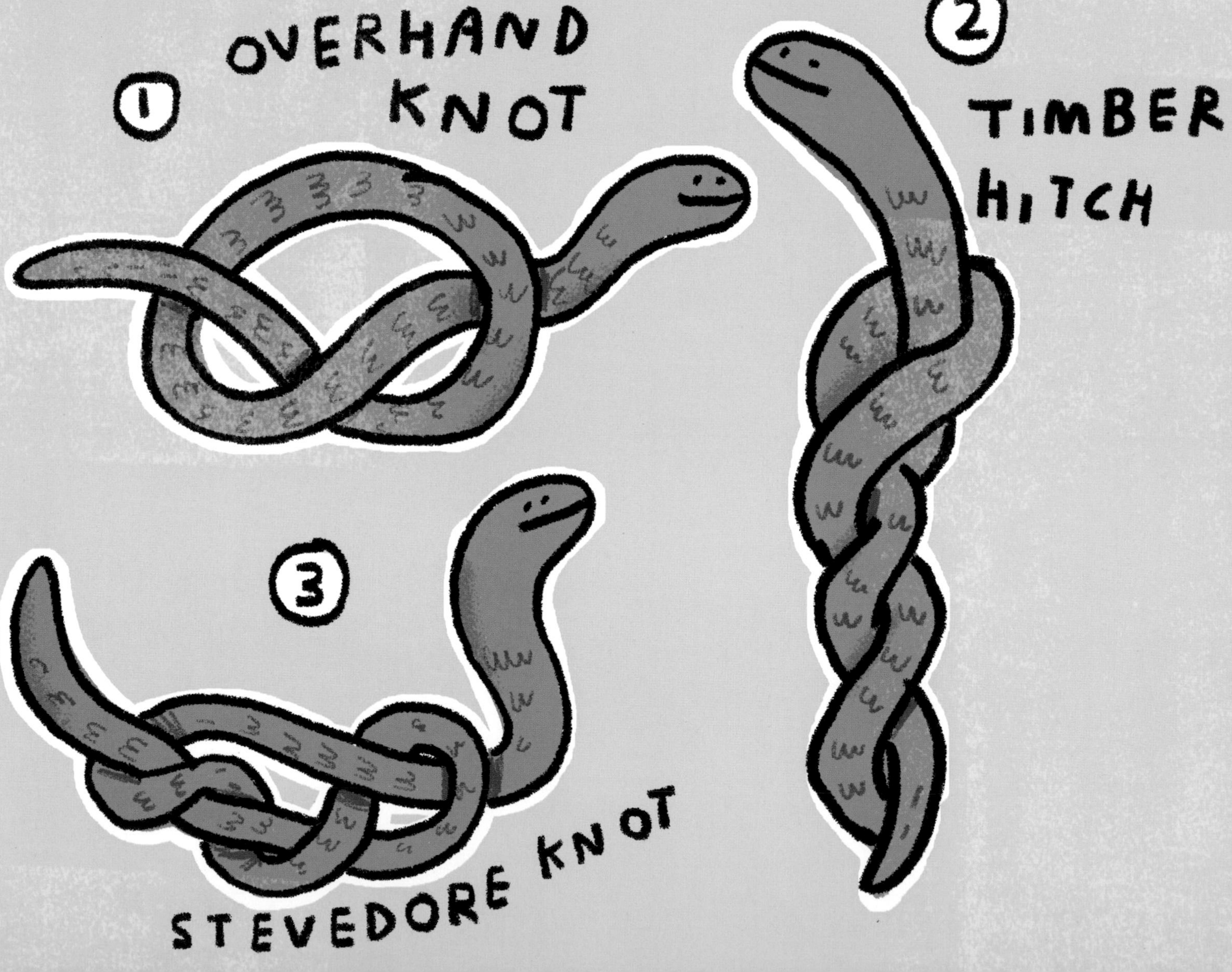

A LOT!
4
FIGURE EIGHT KNOT
5
TWO HALF HITCHES

HIGH FIVE!
BOWLINE KNOT